S.I.P.

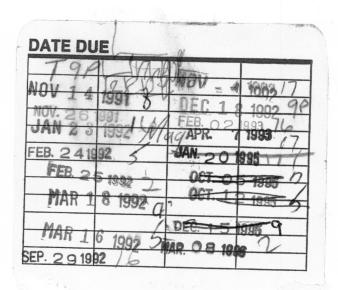

Ralph's Secret Weapon

Story and pictures by STEVEN KELLOGG

Dial Books for Young Readers

New York

EMPIRE GARDENS

Dial Books for Young Readers
A Division of NAL Penguin Inc.
2 Park Avenue
New York, New York 10016

Published simultaneously in Canada by
Fitzhenry & Whiteside Limited, Toronto

Copyright © 1983 by Steven Kellogg
All rights reserved
Library of Congress Catalog Card Number: 82-22115
Printed in Hong Kong by South China Printing Co.
First Pied Piper Printing 1986
COBE
2 4 6 8 10 9 7 5 3

A Pied Piper Book is a registered trademark of
Dial Books for Young Readers,
a division of NAL Penguin Inc.,
®TM 1,163,686 and ® TM 1,054,312.

RALPH'S SECRET WEAPON
is published in a hardcover edition by
Dial Books for Young Readers.
ISBN 0-8037-0024-5

*The process art consists of black line-drawings, black halftones,
and full color washes. The black line is prepared and
photographed separately for greater contrast and sharpness.
The full-color washes and black halftones are
prepared with ink, crayons, and paints on the reverse side
of the black line-drawing. They are then camera-separated and
reproduced as red, blue, yellow, and black halftones.*

For Kevin with love

After successfully completing the third grade Ralph was sent to vacation with his Aunt Georgiana. She greeted him with a banana-spinach cream cake and the news that he would spend the summer learning to play the bassoon.

"This cake is from a recipe that I created myself," said Aunt Georgiana proudly. "I believe in keeping busy," she added, "and I hope that you will study the bassoon with the same energy that I put into all of my projects."

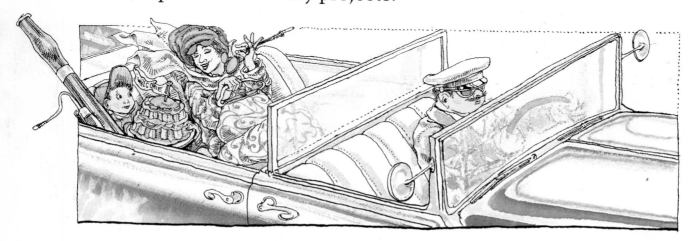

"I'll try," said Ralph.

Aunt Georgiana's house was like a castle. Ralph wanted to explore it and to play with her Great Danes, but she had already planned his afternoon.

"It's important for you to begin practicing immediately," explained Aunt Georgiana. "Your teacher, the famous Maestro Preposteroso, is coming tonight for your first lesson."

Aunt Georgiana left for the afternoon, and Ralph, feeling the need for a snack, went to find the kitchen.

As he entered he saw a mouse nibbling his cake. To his surprise it instantly became very sick.

"I better not eat this thing," Ralph decided, and he hid it in the back of his closet.

During Ralph's first bassoon lesson the sour notes he produced brought worms dancing out of apples.

"He is hopeless. I see no talent whatsoever!" cried the maestro.

"Nonsense!" declared Aunt Georgiana. "He shows great promise as a snake charmer! There is an international snake-charming competition opening at the colosseum tonight, and Ralph and I will be there!" She dismissed the maestro and called for her car.

They arrived just as the snakes were slithering onto the stage and the snake charmers were tuning their instruments.

"What an exciting event!" declared Aunt Georgiana.

Ralph wasn't sure he wanted to sign up.

"Nonsense!" declared his aunt.

Many of the contestants ran into difficulty, but when Ralph played, all the snakes danced to his music.

Ralph's success gave Aunt Georgiana another idea.

Discovering that a sea serpent was causing problems for the navy, she ran to the telephone.

She promised the admiral that her talented nephew would be able to charm the serpent.

The admiral came at once to meet Ralph and to show him slides of the monster in action.

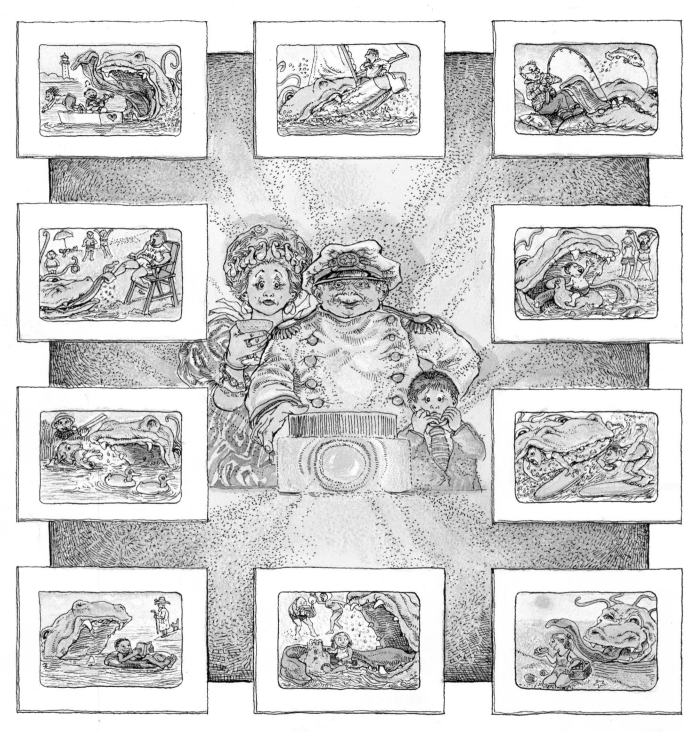

Ralph was worried. He decided that he needed a secret
weapon ready in case of trouble.

Much later aboard the admiral's gunboat Ralph nervously began to play.

Attracted by the music, the monster rose to the surface and snatched the bassoon.

When the music stopped, the sea serpent became angry with Ralph. The crew was frantic. The admiral seemed confused.

"Do something! Save my nephew!" shrieked Aunt Georgiana.

"If we fire, we'll blast Ralph to bits!" wailed the admiral. "What shall we do?"

"Throw my secret weapon!" cried Ralph.

Aunt Georgiana bounded across the deck and flung the bag into the monster's throat.

It sank back making strange burbling sounds.

Suddenly a thunderous hiccup blasted Ralph and the other victims to freedom.

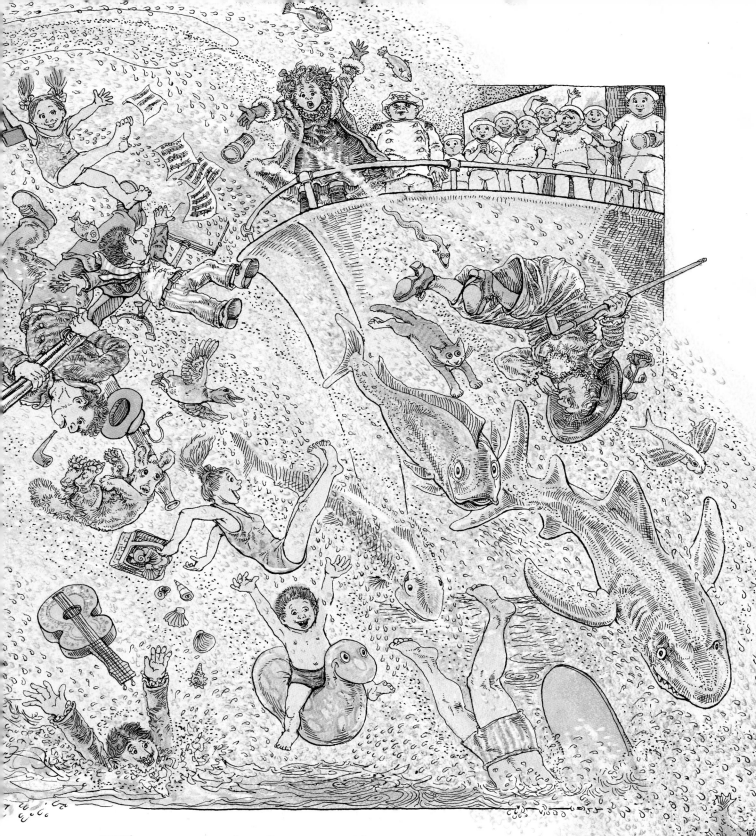

"What was in that bag?" cried Aunt Georgiana.

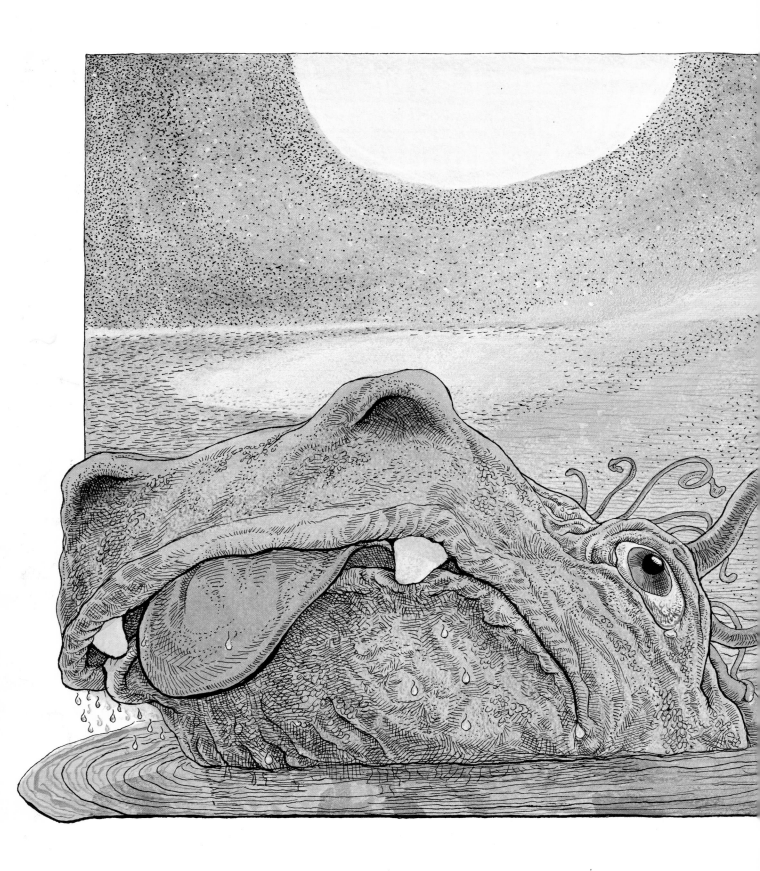

"Your cake," replied Ralph.

When they finally returned home, Aunt Georgiana was exhausted. Ralph was tired too. He announced that he was giving up the bassoon forever.

Aunt Georgiana did not object.

For the rest of the summer Aunt Georgiana kept busy with her projects, while Ralph went swimming, played with the Great Danes, reread his favorite books, and rested up for the fourth grade.